Theories About Continental Drift

STUART STUTZMAN

For Emily.

Contents

Part 1

Feelings

STUART STUTZMAN

Chucks

I saw her there in the geology classroom. She was wearing the same black and white Converse shoes I was wearing. I took this as a sign.

"I like your shoes," I said. She looked down at her shoes and then at mine. She laughed.

"I like yours, too," she said.

"I'm Grant," I said.

"I'm Stephanie," she said.

☐

I don't think you really feel that way

"I think that I have feelings for you," I finally said.

"Really? Why?" Steph asked.

"Because you're great and you understand me and all that."

"Hmm. I don't think you really feel that way."

"What do you mean?"

"I mean, we're really close, and that's great, but I just don't think you see me for who I really am."

"So you don't feel the same about me?"

"I guess not."

The Best Friend You'll Ever Have

"Hey, Steph. You awake?" I asked on the phone. It was about three in the morning.

"I am now," she said. "What's up?"

"I messed up. Is it okay if I come over?"

"I'll unlock the door."

Blood stained the gauze on my arm as I drove across the highway to Steph's apartment. I just walked in when I got there, and Steph was in the kitchen making red Kool-Aid.

"Red's your favorite flavor, right?" she asked me.

"Yeah," I said. The cuts still stung.

She poured us both a glass of Kool-Aid, and we sat down in her bedroom.

Eulogy

"So I've been thinking," I said.

"What's up?" Steph asked.

I put on my turn signal and changed lanes.

"I want you to give my eulogy."

"Umm, okay."

"Well, you know. If anything should happen to me. That's all," I said.

She was silent for a long moment.

"Is anything going to happen to you anytime soon?" she asked.

"I hope not," I said.

Death Cab for Cutie

"Play a Death Cab song!" Steph shouted in her slightly drunk voice. There was no one else awake at the campground, and I didn't want to piss anyone off. "Come on!" she urged.

"Okay," I said. I started to play "I Will Follow You into the Dark" and she cheered.

We woke up next to each other in the tent in the morning after a night of really terrible sleep. Our friend suggested we go back to town to get breakfast tacos.

Best idea ever.

☐

Please don't look at me like that

"Please don't look at me like that," Steph said.

"Like what?" I asked.

"Like I just broke your heart."

Different

"I think in another time and another place we could be something great," Steph said.

"What do you mean?" I asked.

"You know, if things were different, I could definitely see myself growing old with you." Steph was a little drunk. "I mean, you're sweet, handsome, you get me really well, and like...yeah. You're a great guy."

"Okay, drunkie. Let's get you some water." I took her by the hand and started to lead her to the kitchen.

"No, I mean, like, you're awesome and I could do a lot worse. If things were different, I'd be all about that," she said.

"Different how?" I asked.

Steph kissed me on the cheek.

"Just different," she said.
☐

Scars

"How long do you have?" Steph asked.

"Since what?" I asked.

"You know, cutting."

"Three months."

Pause. Steph walked up to me and hugged me, resting her face on my arm where most of my scars are.
☐

Hero

"You know you're like, my hero, right?"

24 Hours

"What if this was your last 24 hours?" I asked her. "What would you do?"

"Would I know it was my last 24 hours?" Steph asked.

"No."

She looked around the dark living room, lit only by the TV, and scooched closer to me on the couch.

"This isn't bad, is it?" she asked.

Hap Hap Happy Birthday!

So drunk.

"Grant! You owe me at least two more shots," Steph slurred at me. "I haven't seen you in forever, and you have to drink more because I haven't seen you in forever."

I grabbed the bottle of tequila and poured another shot. After toasting to something, I downed it and made another tick mark on my arm in Sharpie. The girl I was chasing was gone, and the friend I'd come with was passed out, so it was just Steph, her gay friend, and me doing shots of tequila.

"Uno masmás! Uno masmás!" Steph chanted.

The next morning, I called Steph to ask if she wanted to get breakfast tacos. She was still passed out.

Why do I always get jerks?

"Why do I always end up with jerks?" Steph asked.

"To be fair, you haven't really 'ended up' with anyone," I said.

"You know what I mean."

"Yeah, I know."

She was really frustrated. So was I.

"On behalf of nice guys everywhere," I said. "Please don't give up. You've got a lot of awesome to share, and there are nice guys out there."

"Let me know if you meet any," she said.

Relapse

"I messed up again," I said. I rolled up my sleeve and showed Steph the bandages. Without saying a word, she came up and hugged me.

Pizza

"This is the best pizza in south Austin," I said as we sat in traffic. "It's so worth the wait."

"Okay," Steph said. "Sounds good."

After sitting in traffic for forever, we got to the pizza place. We went in and sat at the counter.

"So I have this talent," Steph said.

"Yeah?"

"Yeah. I can tell a guy I'm only interested in him platonically without telling him that directly," she said.

"Okay..."

"Yeah. Guys never want to hear that, so I've developed a way to tell them that without actually telling them."

"So how do you do that?"

Pause.

"What do you like on your pizza?" Steph asked.

PART II

Sex and Other Terrible Things

STUART STUTZMAN

Mistake

"I think last night was a mistake," she said.

"Okay," I said, thinking I had finally gotten something right.

☐

Fucking

"I wouldn't call it 'making love,'" Steph said. "It was more, like, aggressive."

"Was it fucking?" I asked.

"Yeah, more like fucking."

I didn't like talking about this with her, so I just focused on the chips and queso between us.

I'm Cooler Online Than In Person

"I'm cooler online than in person," Steph said.

"Disagree," I said.   I kept on trying to fill in the questionnaire for the online dating website we were both signing up for.

"Here, look at this picture," Steph said.   She handed me her computer, and I looked at the picture.   I recognized it immediately.   It was a picture of me and her outside a comedy club, but I was cropped out.

"I like that picture," I said.

"Yeah, me too."

Pearl Snap Shirts

"How does this one look?" I asked, holding yet another pearl snap shirt up to me.

"That's my favorite so far. Brings out your eyes," Steph said. "You have nice eyes."

Wheat Beer Is For Vaginas

"Wheat beer is for vaginas," the dude said. Steph was drunk and found this amusing.

I took a sip of my wheat beer and scowled.

Hooking Up

"It's nice to have someone to just hook up with periodically," Steph said.

"I bet," I said. I felt the jealousy rising behind my face, so I just stared down into the bowl of chips sitting between us.

☐

Waffle House

"I'm going to eat all the food," I said. Steph laughed.

Later, in the Waffle House afterglow, Steph's foot brushed against mine.

"Sorry," I said. Steph just smiled.
☐

Firsts

"Do you have tequila?" Steph asked. I walked into the kitchen and looked around in the cabinets.

"We have Jack Daniels and Diet Coke," I said.

"That'll work."

I mixed a Jack and Diet for each of us and went into the living room. Steph was sitting on the couch, so I handed her her drink and sat down on the easy chair.

We sat there, sipping our drinks and chatting about writing until our glasses were empty.

"Come sit with me," Steph said. I got up and sat next to her on the couch. "Thanks for a fun night," she said.

"Anytime," I said.

Then she leaned over and kissed me.
□

Conflict

"I don't like it when you talk like this," Steph said.

So I stopped talking to her.

Hairy Guys Need Love, Too

"He had a bit of a Teen Wolf thing going, but I saw past that," Steph said.

"Hairy guys need love, too," I said.

No One Wants To Hear About Your Drunken Sexploits

"No one wants to hear about your drunken sexploits," Steph said.

"First time in almost seven years. Everyone's going to hear about this," I said.

STUART STUTZMAN

PART III

Goofy Shit

STUART STUTZMAN

South by Southwest

"Sweet Christ, I hate this," I said as I tried to park in the tiny spot on the street.

"Yeah, these people need to go back to California or wherever," Steph said.

"All I want to do is park. That's it."

A car honked at me in the rear view mirror. California plates.

"God, I hate this."
☐

Taylor Swift

"This song makes me think of you," Steph said.

She skipped ahead on the CD to a Taylor Swift song. We drove the next few minutes in silence.

☐

Sean

"I feel like his name will be Sean or something. He'll be of Irish descent, but not weird about it, and he'll be a writer. Me and Sean will go to the bar and drink Jameson until we can't stand straight, and then we'll stagger back to my apartment and watch cartoons and debate the finer points of folk/punk music. He'll look better with a beard than I do, but not by a lot. Then, in the morning, he'll go back and make you breakfast in bed, because he'll be cool like that."

Steph just looked at me.

"What?" I asked. "I've thought a lot about your dream guy. Is that weird?"

Steph just looked at me.

□

Whataburger at 3 a.m.

We were late night people. Or early morning people, depending on who you asked.

"The strength of ordering two different types of taquito is that you can combine them into one Frankentaquito," I said.

"You're a mad man!" Steph said.

I laughed maniacally and took a huge bite of the Frankentaquito.

There was no one else at this Whataburger except the dazed night manager and a cook. Steph and I would sit there until we were almost asleep and talk about whatever came into our minds.

Whataburger at 3 a.m. is a special place.

□

Captain America

It was my 26th birthday, which meant I could no longer be covered by my mother's health insurance.

Adult time.

Steph got me a Captain America piñata for my birthday. The night of my party, she and I and all our friends went outside and beat the shit out of Cap with a legitimate piñata stick.

"Where's the candy?" someone asked after we'd cracked Cap's skull.

"There is no candy. No reward, no nothing. Just like being 26," Steph said with a wry smile.

I hadn't laughed that hard in a long time.
☐

Dedication Page

"I think in my first book, I'll dedicate it to my parents," Steph said.

"My first book will be dedicated to 'everyone who ever put up with me,'" I said. Steph laughed.

"How appropriate."

Moms

"Bullshit!" Steph said. "Your mom adores me!"

"I don't think my mom is capable of adoration," I said.

"Adores, Grant. She adores me."

"What does your mom think of me?" I asked.

"You're alright."
☐

Benjamin

"I'm pretty sure I'm going to have a little boy one day, and I'm going to name him Benjamin," Steph said.

I took a drink and looked out into the night.

"Ben's a good name," I said.

"Not Ben. Benjamin," she said. "He'll be kind of shy and bookish as a kid, but then he'll come into his own in college I think."

"Benjamin sounds like a cool kid," I said.

"Yeah."

Steph took a long drink of her drink and stared off the balcony into the Austin night.

Frito Pie

"My mom's Frito Pie could beat up your mom's Frito Pie," Steph said. I nodded in agreement as I swallowed my beer.

"My mom's a vegetarian. Her Frito Pie is pretty weak."
☐

I'd Be A Great Single Dad

"I think I'd be a great single dad," I said.

"That's kind of sad to think about," Steph said.

"Why?"

"Did your wife die? Did she just leave? What?"

"Does it really matter?"

"I guess not."

I thought for a moment. "The point is I'd be a great single dad. Just me and my kid, doing our best."

Steph smiled a sad smile.

"Yeah. I'd be a great single dad."

Fonts

"I personally am a Times New Roman person," Steph said. "I don't go in for those fancy fonts like Garamond and such."

"I love Garamond!" I said. "It reminds me of a simpler time."

Steph laughed. "When was that exactly?"
☐

Batman

"I always get Batman stuff for my birthday," Steph said.

"Why?" I asked.

"Because he's awesome."

☐

Cat People

"I'm a cat person," Steph said.

"Yeah, I know."

"That doesn't make me crazy, though."

"Not clinically, no."

Proofreading

"Can you proofread this for me?" I asked.

"Sure," Steph said. She was always better at proofreading than me, and took every chance to remind me of that.

"You know that you use semicolons all screwed-ily, right?" she asked after reading for a moment.

"You're a semicolon."
☐

Tattoos

"I'm going to get a tattoo for my grandpa," Steph said.

"That's cool," I said.

"He wouldn't approve of me getting a tattoo in general, but he's dead now. He can deal."

Hype Man

"I would be a great hype man!" Steph said.

"Yeah?"

"Totally! I can solve all your hype and hype related problems."
☐

College Life

"Want to come over for dinner and study time?" Steph asked over the phone.

"Sure," I said.

I put on a clean shirt and headed over to Steph's apartment.

"What kind of ramen do you want?" she asked.

"What do you have?"

"I don't know what the exact flavors are anymore, but one looks brown and the other looks yellow."

I laughed.

"I'm not much of a cook," Steph said.

Texting

"I never texted anyone much before I met you," I said.

"Welcome to the times, Gramps," Steph said.

Voiceover is for Chumps

"My professor said that voiceover was for chumps," I said.

"Then your professor is for chumps!" Steph said. I just stood there. "Steph, one. Your professor, zero."
☐

Plot Holes

"Did you ever notice how in Family Guy Lois is really into theater in the early part of the series and then it's never mentioned again?" Steph asked.

"Nope," I said.

☐

Offspring

"My sister is pregnant…again!" Steph said.

"Stacy's Pregnancy II: The Revenge," I said with a laugh in my movie trailer voice.

"There's no way I'm going to see that movie," Steph said.

"There's no way you can escape it!" I said. "Starring Stephanie Lopez as: The Godmother."

"Rated R," Steph said in her movie trailer voice.

Popeye's or KFC?

"Popeye's or KFC?" I asked. Steph thought for a moment.

"KFC," she said.

"Get out."

PART IV

Long distance is tough

STUART STUTZMAN

What Are You Wearing?

The bar was getting full, and I still didn't see my date. Steph kept texting me from Austin.

"What are you wearing?" she asked.

"Clothes," I replied.

"Take a picture," she said.

I took a quick picture of myself with the camera in my phone and sent it to Steph.

"You look good," she said. "Good luck on your date!"

My date never showed up.

Independence Day

"What did she say?" Steph asked.

"She said no." I said.   Steph put her hand on my shoulder.

"It's probably for the best.   You're here, she's there. Long distance is tough."

I hung my head while fireworks popped in the distance and ice cream melted in my stomach.

"I really liked this one," I said.

"I know," Steph said.

☐

Good at Goodbye

"I wish I wasn't so good at this," I said.

"Good at what?" Steph asked. The moon was full and glittered on the water.

"Saying goodbye."

"We're not saying that. Are we?"

I shrugged.   Steph sat there in silence for a few moments.

"I'm glad you're happy," she finally said.   "Rachel seems really nice."
☐

Bookstores

"I think going to a bookstore with someone is a great second date," Steph said. "I mean, for me at least. I need to know how a given person is going to act at a bookstore."

"I agree," I said.

"Didn't you take Rachel to Half Price Books the other day?" Steph asked.

"Yeah."

"How'd that go?"

"She got bored, so we left and got Starbucks."

"Ouch," Steph said.

"Tell me about it."
☐

Graduation

Steph seemed pretty preoccupied with her family, so I just stood in the background being proud.

☐

STUART STUTZMAN

PART V

Drift

You Still Use Facebook?

"Hey, honey. You'll never guess who I heard from today," I said. Rachel sat down on the bed and turned on the TV.

"Who?" she asked.

"Steph," I said. "She wished me a happy 30th birthday on Facebook."

"You still use Facebook?"

Old People in Love

"That's really sweet," Steph said.

"What?" I asked.

Steph gestured across the parking lot to an old man opening the car door for an old lady.

"Old people in love are the best," she said with a smile.

Poetry

"I'm not much with poetry," I said.

"I've really been getting into it lately," Steph said.

"Yeah?"

"Yeah. It just feels right, you know?"

Pause.

"Do you want to show me any?" I asked.

Steph thought a moment.

"Maybe one day," she said. "When I've got it right, I'll share."

Planning

"We can't invite everyone on this list," Rachel said.

I knew exactly who she was talking about, so I crossed out Steph's name.

Yes We Can

"This is so exciting!" I said as Wolf Blitzer announced another state had gone to then Senator Obama.

"Yeah! We're going to win the first time we voted!" Steph said.

At the end of the night, when he got up and spoke in front of all those people, I looked at Steph and she looked at me. We were sitting there on her couch in Austin and the optimism overwhelmed us. It was a really great feeling.

☐

Rocking the Mic

"Rocking the mic is important," I said. "Especially in these trying times."

Steph laughed as a few more people entered the karaoke bar.

"I'll do a song if you do a song," Steph said.

"Deal."

☐

Austin in the Rain

Steph always thought there was something poetic about the rain, particularly the city in the rain.

Rachel was getting ready for the rehearsal dinner, and I stood out on the porch and watched the rain trickle down out of the clouds. On days like this, Steph and I would sit in her apartment, drink Kool-Aid, and talk about The Dead Poet's Society, but it had been a long, long time since then.

Past Lives

"It's like that episode of The X Files," Steph said. "You know, the one where they talk about reincarnation and how we're always with the same people in each life, just different roles."

"I think I was a traveling salesman or something in a past life. Something very Willy Loman," I said.

"I don't really know what I was," Steph said.

"Do you think we were friends?" I asked.

"I hope so," Steph said. Rain tapped on the window. A comfortable silence elapsed between the two of us as we thought.

"That's a really nice thought," Steph said.

"What?"

"That you're with the same people in each life. Like, you're never really alone."

Theories about Continental Drift

"Hey," Stephanie said. "Come sit with me." It was the second day of class and the professor was actually going to lecture instead of bullshitting about the syllabus.

"Today we're going to talk about continental drift," he said. "It's a pretty simple concept. Basically, the continents drift over the molten part of the earth. Parts of them are destroyed by subduction, but they never really go away, because new earth crust is created, too. The continents move together and apart over millions of years, but they're always there."

Stephanie and I sat there, taking notes and doing our best to listen. Soon, class was over.

"See you next time, Grant," she said with a smile.

"Okay, Stephanie," I said, gathering my books.

"You can call me Steph if you want," she said.

ABOUT THE AUTHOR

Stuart Stutzman is an author who really, really likes nachos. You can write to him at stuartstutzmanlit@gmail.com. He lives and works in Texas.

Made in the USA
Lexington, KY
15 November 2013